WORLD IN VIEW

SPAIN

Nick Caistor

STECK-VAUGHN
LIBRARY
A Division of Steck-Vaughn Company
Austin, Texas

Library of Congress Cataloging-in-Publication Data

Caistor, Nick.
   Spain / Nick Caistor.
     p.   cm.—(World in view)
   "First published by Heinemann Children's Reference
in 1991" — T.p. verso.
   Includes index.
   Summary: Surveys the geography, history, art, economy,
religion, and future of Spain.
   ISBN 0-8114-2450-2
   1. Spain—Juvenile literature. [1. Spain.] I. Title
II. Series.
DP17.C3   1992
946—dc20   91-32573
                                    CIP AC

Cover: *Toledo and the Tagus River, Castille*
Title page: *Llafranch, Costa Brava*

Design by Julian Holland Publishing Ltd.

Typeset by Multifacit Graphics, Keyport, NJ
Printed and bound in the United States by Lake Book,
Melrose Park, IL
1 2 3 4 5 6 7 8 9 0 LB 96 95 94 93 92

Photographic credits
Cover: Robert Everts/Tony Stone Worldwide; title page: J. Allan Cash; 7F Jack Jackson/Robert Harding Picture Library; 8,9 J. Allan Cash; 10 Ronald Sheridan; 11, 13, 16 Navia/Select; 17, 19 Robert Harding Picture Library; 21 Ronald Sheridan; 24 G.M. Wilkins/Robert Harding Picture Library; 26 J. Allan Cash; 28 Bridgeman Art Library; 32 J. Allan Cash; 34 Llenas/Select; 35, 38 Popperfoto; 41 Robert Harding Picture Library; 44 G.R. Richardson/Robert Harding Picture Library; 46 Ronald Sheridan; 48 J. Allan Cash; 51 Xurxo Lobato/Select; 52 Robert Harding Picture Library; 54,55 J. Allan Cash; 58 Navia/Select; 60, 62 Robert Harding Picture Library; 64 Robert Francis/Hutchinson Library; 65 Robert Harding Picture Library; 66 Navia/Select; 68 Baldelli/Contrasto/Select; 71 Robert Harding Picture Library; 74 Robert Francis/Robert Harding Picture Library; 81 Robert Harding Picture Library; 84 Barnabay's Picture Library; 88 Robert Harding Picture Library; 90 Usoz/Select; 92 Popperfoto/Reuter; 93 Mundee/Hutchinson Library.

Contents

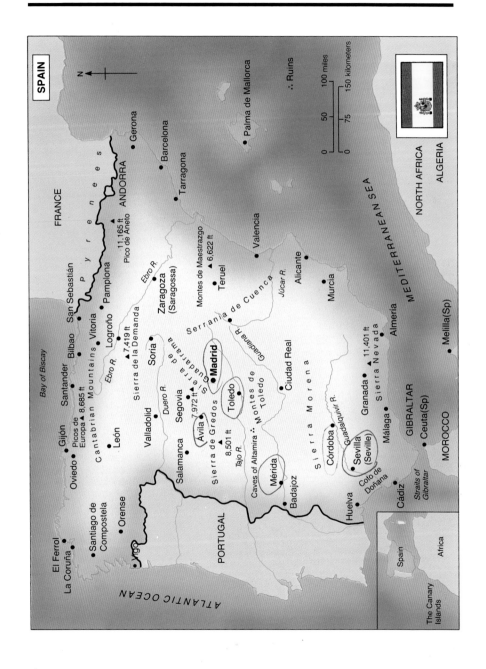

SPAIN

N

FRANCE

ANDORRA

Pyrenees

11,165 ft
Pico de Aneto

Gerona

Barcelona

Tarragona

Bay of Biscay

San Sebastián

Pamplona

Logroño

Vitoria

Bilbao

Santander

Ebro R.

Zaragoza
(Saragossa)

Montes de Maestrazgo

▲ 6,622 ft
Teruel

Valencia

Júcar R.

Alicante

Murcia

MEDITERRANEAN SEA

Palma de Mallorca

∴ Ruins

0   50   100 miles
0   75   150 kilometers

Cantabrian Mountains

Picos de
Europa ▲ 8,685 ft

Gijón

Oviedo

León

Ebro R.

▲ 7,419 ft
Sierra de la Demanda

Soria

Serrania de Cuenca

Guadiana R.

Almería

NORTH AFRICA

ALGERIA

El Ferrol

La Coruña

Santiago de
Compostela

Orense

ATLANTIC OCEAN

Valladolid

Duero R.

Salamanca

Segovia

Sierra de Guadarrama

Madrid

Toledo

Montes de
Toledo

Ciudad Real

Sierra Morena

Granada ▲ 11,401 ft

Sierra Nevada

Málaga

GIBRALTAR

Ceuta(Sp)

MOROCCO

Melilla(Sp)

▲ 7,972 ft
Ávila

Sierra de Gredos

▲ 8,501 ft

Tajo R.

Caves of Altamira ∴

Mérida

Badajoz

Córdoba

Guadalquivir R.

Sevilla
(Seville)

Coto de
Doñana

Huelva

Cádiz

Straits of
Gibraltar

Spain

Africa

The Canary
Islands

PORTUGAL

Vigo

1   Introducing Spain

Spain occupies most of the land known as the Iberian Peninsula. This is the part of Europe that stretches southwest of France, beyond the Pyrenees Mountains. The Pyrenees form a natural border 280 miles (450 kilometers) long, cutting Spain off from France. High in these mountains, the small principality of Andorra perches on the boundary that separates its two large neighbors. To the west, Spain shares a north-south boundary 435 miles (700 kilometers) long with Portugal, the other country in the Iberian Peninsula. To the south lie the Straits of Gibraltar, which divide Spain from Africa and are only 12 miles (20 kilometers) across at their narrowest point. Gibraltar itself, at the mouth of the straits, is an area of 2.3 square miles (6 square kilometers) that belongs to Britain. Spain's closeness to Africa, and the fact that it is cut off from the rest of Europe by the Pyrenees, has given the country a unique history. This shows in the different languages, customs, and ways of life of its people.

Spain is the largest country in western Europe after France. It covers 194,000 square miles (500,000 square kilometers), making it less than eight percent of the size of the United States. Spain is almost square in its shape, measuring between 495 and 560 miles (800 and 900 kilometers) from north to south and east to west. Its northern coastline and the small western one above Portugal both face the Atlantic Ocean, while its southern and eastern coastlines run

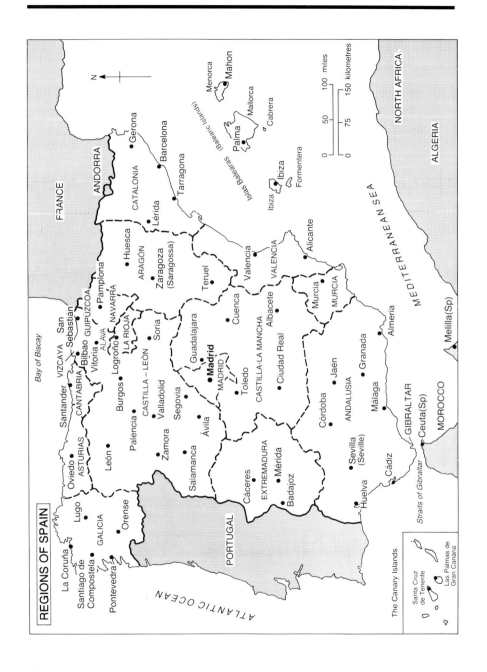

REGIONS OF SPAIN

6

along the Mediterranean Sea. Spain's ocean coasts are rocky and wild, while its sea coasts are far gentler, usually with sandy beaches.

Spain also includes two groups of islands off its coasts. The Canary Islands are in the Atlantic, off the northwest coast of Africa and about 800 miles (1,280 kilometers) from Spain. Only seven of the Canary Islands are inhabited. Volcanic eruptions formed them millions of years ago, and the Pico de Teide on the island of Tenerife is Spain highest mountain at 12,198 feet (3,719 meters). In the Mediterranean off Spain's eastern coast are the five Balearic Islands of Mallorca, Menorca, Ibiza, Formentera, and Cabrera. As well as its islands, Spain controls two cities in Morocco in North Africa—Ceuta and Melilla.

Mallorca is the largest of the Balearic Islands. Its coastline is often rocky, and in some places waves from the Mediterranean have carved out huge caves.

The Cantabrian Mountains border the Bay of Biscay in northwest Spain. It is a very different Spain from the one tourists usually visit but is equally beautiful and has many national parks where the wildlife and the plant life are protected. This is Lake Ercino in the Picos de Europa.

Mountains, meseta, and rivers

Spain is the second highest country in Europe after Switzerland, with an average height of 2,130 feet (650 meters) above sea level. Besides the Pyrenees, which reach 11,155 feet (3,400 meters), Spain has four other main mountain ranges. In the northwest are the Cantabrian Mountains, which include the Picos de Europa. In the center, the Sierra de Guadarrama runs from east to west near the capital, Madrid, while in the south, the Sierra Morena and the Sierra Nevada are snow-clad the whole year round. Between these mountain ranges, almost all of central Spain is a high plateau, or meseta. This plateau dips down near the coasts, where there are strips of fertile lowland, especially on the Mediterranean side of the country.

The Ebro River is Spain's second longest river. It flows 565 miles (910 kilometers) from the Cantabrian Mountains to the Mediterranean Sea.

Spain's five main rivers run across its central plateau. Four of them—the Duero, Tagus (or Tajo in Spanish), the Guadiana, and the Guadalquivir — flow west, into the Atlantic. The Tagus is Spain's longest river and crosses Portugal to reach the ocean at Lisbon, over 620 miles (1,000 kilometers) from its source in the Sierra de Guadarrama. In the north, the Ebro River drains into the Mediterranean south of Barcelona, Spain's second largest city.

Climate
Spain has a variety of temperatures and climates. In the north and west are the region known as the Basque country and Galicia, which are called "green Spain" because winds from the Atlantic Ocean bring rain all year round and keep

9

These are the high plains of the center of Spain. They have produced cereals since the days the Romans lived here. In winter they are bare and very cold, with harsh winds.

temperatures mild in the winter. The temperature at San Sebastián, a town on the coast near the border with France, varies between an average of 74°F (23°C) in the summer months of July and August and 46°F (8°C) in winter. The Mediterranean coasts are drier, with warm summers and mild winters, which make ideal weather for tourists on vacation. Much of the central plateau has meager rainfall, and crops can only be grown with the help of irrigation and water stored in dams. Seville, in the southwest, has less than half the rainfall of San Sebastián, and its average temperature in July and August is 86°F (30°C).

Plant life
The type of vegetation found in Spain varies depending on how high the land is and how much rain it gets. The mountains of the north and west have grassy valleys with woods of poplars, oaks, and other trees that lose their leaves each autumn. Horsechestnut and chestnut trees are

Murcia, in southeastern Spain, is very dry. Much of the mountainous countryside is actually desert where little or nothing will grow. In recent years extensive irrigation has made many parts of Murcia fertile.

also very common. Higher up the slopes, there are large forests of larch and fir, which thin out toward the mountaintops. The mountains of southern Spain have less rainfall, and there the vegetation is mostly tough bushes, with rough, thorny shrubs lower down. The main tree in these parts, and throughout the central plains, is the cork oak, from which cork has been harvested for centuries. On the central plains, people have produced grain for hundreds of years. Where there is more water, grapes and olives grow well. Grapes are cultivated all over Spain except in the northern Basque country.

The most fertile ares of Spain are on the coastal strip of the east and the south, where palm trees and other subtropical plants are typical. Over a

11

Coto Doñana
This national park in the province of Huelva, near Spain's border with Portugal, is a famous nature reserve. Part of it is marshland, where many birds, like the white storks, rest on their migration between Europe and Africa. Another part of the park has bushes and low trees, where many kinds of birds and animals live, such as deer, polecats, wild cats, weasels, and snakes. A third area in the park is covered in pinewoods, which provide a home for wood pigeons, thrushes, rare red kites, eagles, and the azure-winged magpie, which is almost extinct in the rest of Spain. Doñana also has sand dunes, where there are many lizards and snakes, as well as the eagles and owls that eat them.

thousand years ago, Arab invaders from North Africa brought oranges, lemons, figs, and pomegranates to Spain. These fruits have thrived there ever since, because along with them, the Arabs also introduced irrigation systems. The Arabs loved gardens and grew scented flowers, such as carnations, jasmine, and orange-blossom. Where there is no irrigation or rainfall, as in the southeastern region of Murcia, the land is almost desert. Many "Western" movies have been made in this region because it looks very similar to the deserts of the western United States.

Wildlife
One tradition says that the name "Spain" comes from the Phoenician word for "rabbit." The Phoenicians came from the eastern

Mediterranean and founded trading colonies in Spain around 700 B.C. Apparently, when they arrived, they found that the country was full of rabbits. Rabbits, partridge, and other small game still abound in much of the Spanish countryside, and many Spaniards are avid hunters. In more isolated parts of Spain, some larger wild animals

Birds

Birdlife is very rich in Spain. This is because its position between Africa and northern Europe makes it an ideal resting place for millions of birds that migrate each year. Thousands of ducks and geese of every variety fly down from northern Europe to winter on the marshes of Spain. Great flocks of swallows and starlings go even farther, passing over Spain and the Straits of Gibraltar to spend the winter in Africa. Many kinds of birds of prey live in Spain's mountains and isolated highlands. Spain has several types of eagles, including the rare golden eagle. There are also several kinds of vulture, which live in the mountains of the south of Spain.

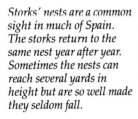

Storks' nests are a common sight in much of Spain. The storks return to the same nest year after year. Sometimes the nests can reach several yards in height but are so well made they seldom fall.

can still occasionally be found. These include brown bear, red deer, wild boar, and the lynx. Very rarely, wolves are also seen. The Spanish mountain goat, or ibex, is quite common, especially in the national parks where wildlife is protected from hunters.

The length of Spain's coastline on the Atlantic and the Mediterranean means that there is a rich animal life offshore as well. Octopus and squid are common in the Mediterranean, particularly around the Balearic Islands. The Atlantic coasts are famous for their schools of sardines and tuna,

---

Spanish Language

As early as the sixteenth century, Spain was divided into 13 mainland regions, plus the Balearic and Canary islands. The regions were different from each other in many ways, including language. The language spoken in Old Castile and New Castile, called Castilian, gradually became the official language for the whole country. It was spoken at court and used in all government and legal documents. People in some of the regions often speak different languages. In Galacia, a part of northwest Spain, the language is called *gallego.* It is similar to Portuguese. In the Basque region, many people still speak the Basque tongue. This is quite different from the other languages of Spain. It is said to be like those found in ancient India! Another language that many people still use is Catalan, spoken in the province of Catalonia. The Valencians who live in the neighboring province speak a similar language, as do the inhabitants of the Balearic Islands.

---

and the dolphins that often appear even in the Straits of Gibraltar.

Population
There are now about 40 million Spaniards. The population is spread very unevenly because of the mountains and the dry plateau in the center of the country. As people have given up farming and left the rural areas, they have moved away from the south and west of Spain to the big cities like Madrid, Barcelona, Valencia, and Seville and to the north. Four out of five Spaniards now live in towns. Madrid has a population of three and a half million, while two and a half million people live in Barcelona. The Mediterranean coastal strip, which is fertile and provides plenty of work, is where the population is most dense.

2   The Making of Spain

Near Avila, in central Spain, are four large granite sculptures. They are known as "the bulls of Guisando." No one knows who made them or what their purpose was, though it is generally thought they were put there by a Celtic tribe several thousand years ago.

The remains of the first people to live in the Iberian Peninsula date back thousands of years. These people lived in caves and used bone and flint tools and weapons to hunt for their food. In several places, such as Altamira and La Pasiega, they painted the walls of their caves with remarkable figures of animals and human beings.

These groups were joined by others who crossed the Mediterranean about 8,000 years ago. Remains of their pottery and the grains they grew have been found on the east coast of Spain and suggest that they were more settled farmers than the other early inhabitants. Celtic tribes came down into Spain from west and central Europe,

bringing their iron working skills and artistic talents to the peninsula. The Phoenicians and the Greeks set up colonies in Spain and traded pottery, metals, and agricultural produce with their home countries. They were the people who introduced olives and grapes into Spain.

Carthaginians and Romans

The Carthaginians, who ruled from their city of Carthage in North Africa, also set up important colonies mainly in the south of Spain. The Romans first came to Spain, which they called "Hispania," during their wars against Carthage in the third century B.C. Over the next 200 years, Rome conquered almost all of the peninsula and unified it by giving it a single government from Rome; a single language, Latin; and, from the

The Romans were expert builders. To bring a regular supply of water to the town of Segovia, they made a channel from the hills of Fuenfria 10.5 miles (17 kilometers) away. They then built this aqueduct of 118 arches made of granite blocks to cross the valley near Segovia. Altogether, the structure is 2,684 feet (818 meters) long, and it still carries water to the town today.

second century A.D., a single religion, Christianity.

The main Roman cities in Spain were along the east coast. The Romans made Tarraco (now Tarragona) their capital. An arch and a small part of the road that led from there to Rome still stand. Many of Spain's roads today follow those first built by the Romans 2,000 years ago. Roman cities housed several thousand people, and the remains of their great amphitheaters, theaters, and temples can still be seen in several places. The Romans in Spain grew wheat to feed the people of Rome, so Spain was known as "the granary of Rome." The Emperor Hadrian, who built Hadrian's Wall along the border between England and Scotland, was born in Hispania, as was the famous writer Seneca and also Pontius Pilate, who condemned Jesus to death.

By the fifth century A.D., Roman rule was crumbling. Tribes from the north of Europe were attacking Italy and Spain. In A.D. 414, one of these tribes, the Visigoths, defeated the Romans and gradually took over the north of Spain. The Visigoth kings adopted Christianity, and many of their churches still stand. The Visigoths are also said to have introduced bullfighting to Spain, but they never managed to unify the country in the way the Romans had.

The Moorish invasion

In A.D. 711, an army of 12,000 Arab troops, known as Moors, crossed into Spain from North Africa. In seven years, they won control of the whole peninsula, except for a small part of the province of Asturias in the north, and some of the remote

Pyrenean valleys. The Arabs called Spain "Al-Andalas." They stayed for eight centuries and changed the country as profoundly as the Romans had done before them. The Arab religion was Islam, whose followers were called Muslims, and at first Spain was part of the Muslim empire. It was controlled from Damascus, but within a century it was an independent Arab kingdom, with its capital in Córdoba. The Arabs not only brought with them their Muslim religion but also

When it was built, over 1,200 years ago, the mosque at Córdoba was the most important one in the western Islamic world. There are 856 horseshoe arches, a typical feature of Arab architecture. When the Christians reconquered Córdoba in 1236, they turned the mosque into a cathedral, covering the roof and building a tall belltower.

new learning in mathematics and the sciences, and new crops, like cotton, sugarcane, dates, oranges, and lemons. Their great love of horses also became part of the Spanish tradition, as did games such as chess. Their architecture was very different from that of the Romans, with rounded arches, painted tiles, and brickwork rather than stone. They were expert potters and glassmakers too.

Over the centuries, the Arabs intermarried with the Spanish people, creating a new kind of mixed society. They were also tolerant of Jewish people, so that about 800 years ago a city like Toledo had thriving Arab, Christian, and Jewish traditions. Many town names, especially in the south of Spain, are Arabic in origin. "Gibraltar," for example, comes from *gebel Tarik*, "the rock of Tarik,"named for one of the first invaders. The Spanish language also has many words of Arabic origin, which often begin with *al-*, such as *algodón*, cotton, *almuerzo*, lunch, and *albergue*, hostel. A handful of Arabic words, such as "azure," "nadir," and "zenith," has passed into English. These particular words are all related to astronomy, a science in which the Spanish Arabs were very skilled.

The Christian reconquest
The Arabs never conquered the whole of Spain. The tiny Christian kingdoms of Asturias and Aragón began to fight back almost at once, but they only reconquered Muslim Spain very slowly because they often fought among themselves as well. By the fourteenth century they had recovered Córdoba, Seville, and Cádiz, an

THE MAKING OF SPAIN

As the Christians advanced south across Spain, they built castles to defend the territory they had captured. This castle at Ponferrada was built in the thirteenth century by the Knights Templar. The names of the kingdoms of Castile and New Castile come from all the castles built there.

important port on the south coast of Spain. The main remaining Arab kingdom was centered on Granada, with its magnificent palace, fortress and gardens of the Alhambra. In the Middle Ages, Castile and Aragón became the two most powerful Christian kingdoms and the focus for attack on Arab lands. One of the most famous Christian warriors was El Cid, who fought for the king of Castile against the Arabs in the eleventh century. He captured Valencia on the east coast but later quarreled with his king. He lived in exile for many years but was finally forgiven and returned to fight once more. An epic poem, *El Cantar del Mío Cid*, was written about him one hundred years later. This is one of the earliest works of literature in the Spanish language.

The Way to Santiago de Compostela
An early Christian legend has it that the body
of St. James the Apostle *(Santiago)* was
brought to Spain after his death in A.D. 44. In
813, his remains were rediscovered at
Compostela in northwest Spain. A shrine was
built to him, which later became a cathedral,
and St. James became the patron saint of
Spain. He was said to appear miraculously
when the Spaniards were fighting the Arabs.
Millions of pilgrims from all over Europe made
their way to the shrine at Santiago de
Compostela, often wearing the scallop shell
that was their emblem. Towns grew up along
the route the pilgrims took down from the
Pyrenees across northern Spain. Thousands
of Christians still visit the cathedral of
Santiago de Compostela every year to rub the
knee of the saint's statue, which is the
traditional way of receiving his blessing.

In 1469, Isabella, the young queen of Castile,
married Ferdinand, king of Aragón. They were
both determined that they would drive the Arabs
out of Spain completely, and their success earned
them the title of "the Catholic kings." Ferdinand
and his warriors fought every year, reducing the
Arab territory around the city of Granada. Finally,
in 1492, after almost 600 years, Granada
surrendered to the Catholic kings, and Spain was
once again united under the Christian rule.

There were, however, many Jews and some
Arabs still living in the country. In 1478,
Ferdinand and Isabella had set up the Inquisition
to investigate how genuine people's Catholic
belief really was, especially that of Jews who had

been newly converted. In 1492, the Catholic kings forced all the Jews who would not become Catholics to leave Spain. The Muslims were also expelled, the last of them leaving in 1609.

The year 1492 is also significant as the year an Italian explorer named Christopher Columbus discovered America. He had persuaded Queen Isabella to finance his journey in search of a new route to India. Sailing westward, he thought he had achieved his goal when he found land, but in fact, what he had landed on was one of the Bahama Islands in the West Indies. He called it San Salvador. Columbus made three more voyages but died thinking he was exploring new lands in the Far East. Early in the sixteenth century, other Spanish explorers discovered the mainland of the Americas. This discovery, and the conquest that followed it, brought Spain a vast new empire, which made it the richest and most powerful nation in Europe.

3   Empire and Decline

Christopher Columbus returned to Seville in 1493 after his first voyage of discovery, and Seville soon became Spain's main port for trading with the Americas. The administration of the colonies took place in the House of the Indies, and this tower was called the Tower of Gold (Torre del Oro) because all the gold from the colonies passed through it.

The Spanish adventurers, or *conquistadores*, gradually conquered Mexico, much of Latin America, and large parts of what is now the United States. A decree from the Pope stated that these lands could become part of a Spanish empire if the Spaniards took the Christian religion with them. So, as they won new territory from the people originally living there, the Spaniards converted them to Catholicism. Other Spanish colonies were founded in the Pacific in Guam and the Philippines. Poor soldiers from rural Spain became owners of huge areas of land in the new colonies. Jewels, gold, and other

precious metals and goods were shipped back from the Americas to the Spanish ports of Seville and Cádiz. The colonies could only trade with Spain, which meant that Spain grew very rich but also isolated, because in developing links with its colonies it turned away from the rest of the world.

The Hapsburg dynasty

Spain was also very powerful in Europe. Isabella and Ferdinand had no surviving sons, but their daughter Juana married into the Hapsburg family, who were rulers of the Holy Roman Empire. In 1519, the grandson of the Catholic kings, Charles, found himself wearing two crowns. He was not only Charles I of Spain but also Charles V of Austria, Holy Roman Emperor, ruling the Netherlands and much of Italy and Germany as well. He was the ruler who decided that Madrid was to be the capital of Spain. He chose it to weaken the traditional power of the provinces, and to show he was the absolute ruler. Charles spent almost 40 years fighting other European countries as well as the Turkish empire, before abdicating in 1556 to live out his last years in a monastery.

This religious gesture was typical of the strength of Catholicism in Spain. Spain produced many devout Catholics. Saint Teresa of Avila set about reforming the Carmelite order of nuns and founded a whole network of convents for them, in addition to writing her autobiography and many mystical religious works. Her companion was St. John of the Cross, who also wrote mystical poetry. In 1534, another man who became a saint, Ignatius de Loyola, created what

King Philip II built the vast monastery of El Escorial outside Madrid as a burial place for his father, Charles V. It took 22 years to finish and was not completed until 1584. The monastery was dedicated to St. Laurence and is made in the shape of the gridiron on which the saint was burned alive. Built of gray granite, its severe classical style is typical of the religious faith and grandeur of sixteenth-century Spain.

The Golden Age in the Arts

Under Philip II, Spanish literature and painting enjoyed its golden age. Pedro Calderón de la Barca and Lope de Vega wrote plays that are still performed, while Luis de Góngora and Quevedo wrote fascinating poetry. Among the artists who painted religious, courtly, and everyday subjects were Velázquez, Murillo, and El Greco. The novelist Miguel de Cervantes Saavedra wrote his book *Don Quixote de la Mancha* between 1605 and 1615, creating one of the greatest characters in world literature. Don Quixote spends his life trying to be like the knights he has read about in books. He dreams of noble deeds and fantastic exploits but usually makes himself look ridiculous. His constant companion is his servant, Sancho Panza, who is down-to-earth and realistic.

he called the Society of Jesus, also known as the Jesuits. They became the great teachers of religion throughout the Spanish empire.

Charles' son, Philip II, continued the task of ruling the huge empire. In 1554, he married the Catholic Mary Tudor of England but only lived in England for one year. Mary's successor, the Protestant Elizabeth I, became his enemy. English ships attacked the rich towns in Spanish America and the galleons bringing back the colonies' wealth to Spain. So, in 1588, Philip tried to crush England by sending a great fleet, or armada, to invade it. The attempt ended in disaster, with up to 30,000 men and 160 ships lost.

The break-up of the empire

Philip II died at the very end of the sixteenth century, in 1598. The next 200 years saw the slow decline of Spain's power. It still drew immense riches from its colonies in the Americas, but in Europe it lost control of the Netherlands, and Portugal broke free once more. Britain, Holland, and France were more active in trade and agriculture and were also starting to create industries to mass-produce goods, while Spain continued with the same systems of farming, trading, and administration.

The eighteenth century began with the nations of Europe fighting a lengthy war, the War of the Spanish Succession (1701–14). Its purpose was to keep the French kings from taking over the Spanish throne after Philip II's great-grandson died without leaving an heir. Austria won Spain's possessions in the Netherlands and Italy, and the British took Gibraltar and Menorca. In the end,

*Francisco de Goya
(1746–1828) began as a
court painter, but when the
French took over Spain in
1808, he turned to
drawing the terrible scenes
of cruelty and suffering
that he saw all around
him. This painting shows
a riot that took place in
Madrid on May 2, 1808.*

Philip of Anjou, grandson of Louis XIV of France, came to the throne of Spain as Philip V, and for one hundred years Spain was closely allied to France. This encouraged the development of the northern part of the country, so the first industries started in the provinces of Catalonia, Valencia, and Asturias.

By the end of the eighteenth century, Spanish rule over its colonies in the Americas was weakening. The colonies wanted independence like the U.S., and the power to trade with other countries besides Spain, such as Britain and Holland. The kings of Spain were weak and could not stop Spain's decline. Many people in Spain

admired the new ideas about democracy that were springing up in France and supported the French Revolution when it took place in 1789. They wanted to get rid of the monarchy and its privileges in Spain and set up a republic where the people or their representatives could govern instead. In 1808, Napoleon invaded Spain, and Spanish patriots rose against the French. The Church and those who supported the Spanish monarchy led the opposition, which meant that those who favored republican ideas were seen as antipatriotic. In 1813, the British Duke of Wellington drove the French troops out of Spain and went on to defeat Napoleon two years later.

After Napoleon's defeat, the Spanish monarchy was restored under Ferdinand VII. At first, he did not want to give any power to a parliament or the people. There were frequent uprisings and much blood was shed, particularly in the northern regions, where the people resented control from Madrid. Spain had already lost most of its overseas empire, except for the Philippines, Cuba, and Puerto Rico. All the other Spanish colonies in the Americas had won their independence.

Monarchy and republic
Ferdinand VII died without a male heir. His daughter Isabella was under age, and so Ferdinand's brother, Don Carlos, claimed the throne. The first of what were known as the Carlist Wars for the throne broke out in 1833, between traditional supporters of the monarchy, who backed Don Carlos, and more liberal reformers who backed Isabella. For the next 40

years, there was fighting between the two factions. This was aggravated as various regions joined the Carlists to defend their own traditions. In 1869, there was a revolution that forced Queen Isabella to give up the throne. A provisional government was set up during which Spain's first real parliamentary constitution was passed. In 1873, the first Republic was proclaimed. This lasted less than a year, after which Isabella's son was made king. In 1902, King Alfonso XIII came to the throne.

During World War I, Spain remained neutral, but its internal troubles led General Primo de Rivera to stage a coup against the king in 1923. Alfonso stepped down, and the general ruled as dictator for six years. Although the king came back in 1929, it was not long before the parliament and organized workers were demanding that he

The Decline of Spain

Throughout the nineteenth century, Spain's population grew more slowly than that of its European neighbors. In 1900, there were less than 20 million Spaniards, only half the size of France's population. Almost 90 percent of these Spaniards still worked on the land. What industry there was became concentrated in the north of the country, around the iron and coal deposits of the Basque Provinces, or along the coastal strip of Catalonia and Valencia. Spain's international status also fell as it lost the last possessions it had to the United States, handing over first Puerto Rico, then the Philippines and Guam, and finally, in 1898, the island of Cuba, which had been ruled by the Spaniards for almost 400 years.

go. In 1931, the Republicans and Socialists came to power in the parliamentary elections. Alfonso was forced to step down, and Spain's second Republic was formed.

The Second Republic
The Republicans tried to introduce reforms to break up the huge estates that belonged to the landed gentry in Andalusia in the south of Spain. They also tried to limit the powers of the Church and granted some self-rule to Catalonia and the Basque Provinces. These measures worried the right-wing and Catholic groups, so in the next elections of 1933, these conservatives came to power. The 1930s saw political parties in Spain, as in the rest of Europe, becoming increasingly extreme. The son of the dictator Primo de Rivera set up a far-right-wing Fascist party called the Falange. He based it on the Fascist party that Mussolini had founded in Italy in 1919. The Anarchists, who did not believe in a central government and wanted power for the trade unions, were strong in Catalonia. In addition to the Socialists, there was a strong Communist party, in cities like Madrid, Bilbao, and Barcelona.

In the next elections, in 1936, the Popular Front, made up of the Republicans, Socialists, and Communists, won a large majority in parliament. Some Anarchists and Socialists thought the moment for a popular revolution had come. There were battles between them and the Falangists, and many attacks on the Church. On July 18, 1936, a group of army officers rebelled against the Republican government. This was the start of a civil war.

4

War, Franco, and a New Spain

At the head of the uprising against the Republican government was General Francisco Franco y Bahamonde. He had been in charge of Spanish troops in the Canary Islands and Morocco and now flew in with his army. Most of the armed forces remained faithful to the Republic, but the uprising was successful in many regions, especially the country areas of the south and west of Spain. Almost overnight, Spain was split into two. A civil war began that was to last for three years.

The alcázar, *or fortress, of Toledo was a symbol of the heroism of the Nationalist troops during the civil war. The city of Toledo was held by the Republicans, but the soldiers in the alcázar were supporters of Franco. From July to September 1936, the Republicans attacked the fortress, but the men inside held out. Finally Nationalist troops attacked the city and relieved the garrison.*

The triumph of the nationalists

General Franco and his supporters called themselves the Nationalists, claiming they represented the true Spain. They soon won over almost half the country. The Nationalists were much better organized than the Republicans, whose army was made up of many different groups that sometimes fought each other for control. So, General Franco's troops gradually gained the upper hand, winning more and more territory. When they conquered the rich industrial regions of the Basque Provinces in 1938, their victory became certain. The

---

The Civil War 1936–39
The fiercest battle of the civil war was for the capital, Madrid. In the winter of 1936–37, Franco tried for many months to capture it. His troops even reached the suburbs but never managed to take the city. This was because the Republican army defended it so bravely, with the help of volunteers who came from many other countries to aid the Spanish government. These foreign volunteers were mainly Communist sympathizers (about 20,000) and fought in International Brigades alongside the Republican troops. The Soviet Union also sent weapons and supplies to the Spanish Communists and the Republican government. The Nazis in Germany, under Hitler, and Fascists in Italy, under Mussolini, sent help to the Nationalists. In 1939 Madrid was captured and the Nationalists won. The civil war ended on March 31, 1939. The war in Spain, which took about 750,000 lives, was a great international cause that divided the sympathies of people all over the world.

On April 26, 1937, German planes supporting the Nationalists bombed the Basque town of Guernica. Many hundreds of civilians were killed, including women and children. The Spanish painter, Pablo Picasso, who was living in France, painted this emotional picture of the bombing to express his horror at the idea of innocent people being killed. Picasso refused to let his painting be shown in Spain until Spain had true democracy. For many years it was hung in a museum in New York, but it was finally taken to Madrid in 1987.

Republicans tried to counterattack in the spring of 1939, but when their attempt failed, they were forced to surrender. More than half a million Spaniards had died in three years' fighting. Half a million supporters of the Republican side became refugees and fled to France, Britain, and Latin America, because they were afraid that they would be imprisoned or shot by the victorious Nationalists.

Francoism

Although General Franco had been only one of the several generals in the 1936 uprising, by 1939 he was the unchallenged leader of the Nationalists. After the war, he made himself head of state and he was known as Caudillo, or the leader of the nation. He only allowed the existence of one political party, which, of course, supported him, and he shut down parliament. Instead of forgiving the Republicans, who made up nearly half the country's population, his government harshly punished them. Even when

General Franco opened this huge monument in the Valley of the Fallen in 1959. It was erected 25 miles (40 kilometers) outside Madrid to the memory of Nationalists who died during the civil war. Many Spaniards objected that it did not commemorate the thousands of Republicans who had also died, sincerely believing in their own ideals. Franco's remains were brought here to be buried in 1975.

Spain officially became a monarchy again in 1947, General Franco held almost all the power.

Catalonia and the Basque Provinces, which had governed themselves during the Republic, were brought back under the central control of Madrid. The 1940s were extremely hard for everyone in Spain. They became known as the years of hunger, or *años de hambre*, because there was a shortage of everything. As many as 250,000 people died of hunger or poor living conditions in the years immediately after the civil war.

During World War II, Spain kept out of the fighting. After the defeat of Hitler and Mussolini, General Franco and Salazar in Portugal stood alone as the only two right-wing dictators left in

Europe. Franco was determined to be independent of all the other countries and to take Spain along the path he wanted to follow. As in earlier centuries, this meant that Spain was cut off from the rest of Europe. While other European countries were settling down into democracy and prosperity in the 1950's, life in Spain was very much the same as it had been a century earlier. Franco believed in strict Catholicism, encouraging people to accept their sufferings instead of trying to stop them. For him, society depended on the family, in which the man was head of the household. Any protests or strikes were dealt with very harshly. There was little respect for free speech, and newspapers, the radio and television had to agree with his political views. Franco also had the idea that the male head of the family should control everything: women and children needed his permission to have a job, a bank account, or to travel outside Spain. Franco encouraged the role of the Catholic Church in teaching strict ideas of good and evil.

Change and growth

By the end of the 1950's, it was becoming very hard for Spain to remain isolated, so it made a remarkable attempt to modernize its methods of production and create new industries. The industrial boom changed Spain more than anything else had done in the previous hundred years. Many thousands of people left the countryside, especially in the poor and undeveloped south and west, and went to look for work in Madrid and the towns and cities of Catalonia and the Basque Provinces. This huge movement of population created fresh problems in the cities, where there was no place for people to live. It also produced large groups of workers, who formed themselves into unofficial unions run by the Communists to demand good conditions from their employers. Students and intellectuals, who traveled abroad, learned of a very different world outside of Franco's Spain. There was also regional pressure on the centralized Franco regime. In Catalonia, protests against rule from Madrid helped make Catalans aware of how suppressed their own culture was. In the Basque Provinces, some groups turned to terrorism, shooting, kidnapping, and bombing, to make people aware of their demand for independence.

The end of the regime
Even in the 1970s, General Franco still thought his kind of Spain could survive him. He had decided that the best way of bringing this about was to appoint a king as head of state to succeed him. This would keep political parties from returning to power. He was aware that Don Carlos, who was the son of Alfonso XIII and the heir to the throne, had not supported him during the civil war. He therefore chose Don Carlos's son, Juan Carlos, as the next king of Spain. Franco took charge of the education and military training of Juan Carlos at an early age. He was sure that Juan Carlos would continue to uphold Francoism.

The transition to democracy
Franco died in November 1975, after almost 40 years in power. As his successor, Juan Carlos

The Spanish royal family in the Cortes after the swearing-in ceremony for King Juan Carlos in 1975. King Juan Carlos married Princess Sofia of Greece in 1962. They have three children—two girls, Elena and Cristina, and one boy, Felipe. Felipe, born in 1968, is now heir to the Spanish throne.

proved to be a very different ruler than Franco had expected. He called on a capable politician, Adolfo Suárez, to be prime minister. Suárez was not left-wing or right-wing but had more moderate views of the center. The king and Suárez immediately set about consulting all the administrative sectors in Spain about the sort of government they wanted. Trade unions, political parties, and social organizations all gave their views. There was also to be a new constitution, for although Spain would not go back to being a republic, people wanted a constitutional monarchy, like that of Britain or the Netherlands. In many ways, the new Spain was growing closer to its European neighbors.

Las Cortes
The Spanish parliament is called the *Cortes Generales* and meets in Madrid. It has two houses, the Chamber of Deputies and the Senate. All Spaniards over the age of 18 can vote. The political party or group that has the most members elected then forms a government whose leader becomes the prime minister.

In June 1977, Spaniards voted freely for the first time since 1936. There was no violence. They chose Suárez and the group of central parties in the UCD (Democratic Center Union) that he represented to take power in the new *Cortes Generales*, or parliament. Suárez then began to bring Spain into line with the rest of Europe. Some of the armed forces did not like the speed of these political changes, and in February 1981, they staged a coup in the Cortes. They wanted to force the king to take power and dismiss all the politicians.

King Juan Carlos refused, and because the majority of the armed forces stayed loyal to him, parliamentary democracy survived. Since then, the armed forces have accepted the authority of the king and of the politicians. The UCD lost to the PSOE (Spanish Socialist Workers' Party) in the 1982 elections, and the PSOE has been in power ever since. They are far from being left-wing Socialists as their party title suggests, but are much more moderate.

To solve the old problem of Spain's regions resenting the central control of Madrid, the country has been divided into 17 self-governing areas, 14 of which are on the mainland. These areas have their own parliaments and regional governments. They now make their own decisions about aspects of regional life like education, health, and planning. Spain has become, in fact, more of a federal state like the United States.

Joining the European Community
In 1986, Spain became a full member of the European Community (EC). This meant that Spain was finally on a par with France, Italy, and the rest of Europe. Spain's industry and economic growth now matched that of its European competitors, and politically, it was a stable democracy. After 1992, Europe's free market with no trade barriers will put Spain's new role as a European country to the test. It is an historic coincidence that Spain takes it place in Europe in the same year that it is celebrating the five hundredth year of its discovery of the Americas. Spain is looking to the future while remembering its past.

5 Madrid, Barcelona, and the Regions

The city of Madrid is in the center of Spain. The fact that it is on a plateau 2,150 feet (655 meters) above sea level and a long way from the coast make its climate very extreme. In winter, the temperature can be as low as 10°F (-12°C), while in the summer it can rise to 104°F (49°C). People have described Madrid's climate as "nine months of winter and three months of hell."

The Calle de Alcala is one of the busiest roads into the center of Madrid.

A thousand years ago Madrid was the small Moorish town of Majrit. It was retaken by the Christians in the twelfth century. For many years

41

Toledo was the capital of Christian Spain, and although Charles V changed the capital to Madrid, it was not until the reign of his son Philip II that the court moved there in 1561, largely for political reasons. Since then, Madrid has always been the political center of Spain, but because it was not near the sea or any large rivers and did not have any significant mineral deposits nearby, it did not grow as quickly as other cities, such as Barcelona.

In the nineteenth century, however, Madrid became the railroad hub of the country. The development of modern roads also helped the capital to develop as an industrial center as well as an administrative center. There are now over three million inhabitants in the capital. Unlike other European capitals, such as Paris or London, it is not surrounded by miles of suburbs that house more people. The countryside around Madrid is quite empty because it rises quickly into mountains where the weather is very harsh.

Madrid has many sights to see because of its past as the center of an empire. The royal palace and its gardens are an elegant reminder of the eighteenth century. The Prado Museum is one of the finest classical art galleries in the world, while behind it, the gardens of the Parque del Retiro are a favorite for strollers and families. At night, the narrow streets of the old part of the city come alive, as the many bars and restaurants stay open until the early hours of the morning for their customers. The people of Madrid, called *Madrileños*, consider themselves the purest-bred Spaniards. Their language, Castilian, was the one that united the whole country and eventually all the Spanish empire. With the court and the national parliament based in the city, the people of Madrid have always felt at the forefront of Spain's politics, culture, and fashion. Today, Madrid is the base for Spain's main national newspapers, Spanish television, and the offices of many international companies.

Barcelona
There is a constant rivalry between Madrid and the second largest city in Spain, Barcelona. Although its population of two million inhabitants is smaller than that of the capital, the inhabitants of Barcelona think their city has a much richer history than Madrid. They also pride themselves on being more open to influence from the rest of Europe. Most of Barcelona's inhabitants speak Catalan, the language of Catalonia, in preference to Castilian Spanish.

Barcelona, on the Mediterranean coast, has been a port for 2,000 years. It was used by the Iberians, and it became an important town under the Romans. Beginning in the ninth century, the counts of Barcelona ruled independently, and when Catalonia and Aragón united in the twelfth century, Barcelona became one of the most powerful cities on the Mediterranean. Many of its impressive monuments, such as the cathedral, date from this period. After the death of King Ferdinand in the sixteenth century and the discovery of the Americas, Barcelona began to decline because trade with the new colonies centered on Seville in the southwest.

As industry grew in Europe in the nineteenth century, new life returned to Barcelona. It was

The city of Barcelona is built on a strip of land between the Mediterranean and the mountain range of Tibidabo. It has been an important port for over 2,000 years.

closer to France and Italy than Madrid and so was able to take the lead in exporting and importing goods. At the end of the nineteenth century, the city enjoyed a new boom, which was reflected in the architectural creation of people like Antoni Gaudí. Barcelona's economic strength, together with a strong sense of the cultural differences between Catalans and Castilians, made many people in Catalonia impatient to regain their independence. They achieved home rule under the Republic in the 1930s, and Catalonia strongly supported the Republican cause in the Spanish civil war. Barcelona was the last major city to fall to Franco's Nationalist troops.

Under Francoism, Barcelona and Catalonia paid for their Republicanism. Schools were forbidden to teach Catalan, and all publications had to be in Castilian, the official language. Government money and new jobs went to other regions. Once more, though, as Spain opened up to Europe in the 1950s and 1960s, it was Barcelona that benefited. The region now enjoys self-government again, and the city of Barcelona was chosen to host the Olympic Games in 1992. The vast majority of Catalans still see themselves as Catalans first and Spaniards second but can accept that they are both.

The Basque Provinces
In the three Basque Provinces of the north, Alava, Guipúzcoa, and Vizcaya, this question of identity causes serious problems. The Basques are very proud of their traditions. Many of them feel that the Basque language, their history, and the fact that they are fair-skinned, not dark like most other Spaniards, makes them not just a different region but a different nation. This nation would also include parts of southwest France.

Basque Nationalists
A group called ETA *(Euskadi Ta Askatasuna,* meaning "Basques and Freedom") frequently challenges the authority of Madrid over the Basque Provinces. Besides fighting for their views politically, they plant bombs, shoot policemen, and kidnap people to pressure the Spanish government into letting them manage all their own affairs. As in other regions, the government has given the Basques control over many issues that affect them directly, like education and health. The majority of Basques seem happy with this, but ETA continues to fight for more.

The Basque Provinces have lush green countryside with wooded valleys, meadows, and many fruit trees. But for many years there has also been heavy industry, based on iron ore deposits and timber. This industry makes the cities of the Basque Provinces, like its main port of Bilbao, both very busy and very dirty. The long Basque coastline has also made it a region of explorers and fishermen. Sebastián Elcano, who in 1522 completed the first voyage around the world after Magellan was killed, was a Basque. The fish and the rich farmland of the Basque Provinces make them one of Spain's richest regions for cooking. The Basques are also famous in Spain for their passion for sports and gambling.

Farms in Galicia tend to be small because they have been divided up by each generation of farmers. The farms produce corn and vegetables, while on the hills the farmers keep sheep, pigs, and horses. This is often barely enough to feed the farm family.

Galicia

Farther around the northwest of Spain, the Galicians have their own language. The Galician Provinces border on Portugal, and the Galician language, which is still spoken by several thousand people, is similar to Portuguese. Like

the Portuguese and the Basques, Galicians are
great sailors. Spain's main port in Galicia is Vigo,
and trawlers sail from it to fish all over the
Atlantic. This is part of "green Spain," which
receives over 60 inches (150 centimeters) of rain
per year. The result is rich agricultural land,
where the Galicians grow corn and other cereals.
There are also many apple trees, and this is one of
the few regions in Spain where cider is the local
drink rather than wine.

Despite these natural riches, the provinces of
Galicia have always been poor. For hundreds of
years, Galicians were forced to emigrate to find
work. They crossed the Atlantic by the thousands
to live and work in Latin America, especially in
Argentina. More recently, they have gone to work
in Germany or other parts of Europe. Being away
from their country gives Galicians a special kind
of homesickness that is reflected in their poetry
and their music, which is played on bagpipes.

Andalusia

For many visitors to Spain, it is Andalusia in the
south that typifies the whole country.
Andalusia's inland cities, like Córdoba, Seville,
and Grenada, were the great capitals of Moorish
Spain and have a distinct atmosphere all of their
own. The people are small, dark-haired and
brown-eyed, like their Arab ancestors. Their
houses are often painted white to keep them cool
in the fierce summer sun. Decorative ironwork
grilles protect their windows, and inside they
have tiled patios full of flowers—all part of the
Arab tradition.

Although the land in Andalusia's river valleys

These white houses in Mijas on the Costa del Sol are typical of Andalusia. They are whitewashed every year. The white paint reflects the sun's rays, keeping the inside of the houses cool in the very high temperatures of the summer.

is fertile, producing grapes and citrus fruits, only a small number of landowners control it, so that many people from Andalusia have also been obliged to migrate abroad or to other parts of Spain to find work.

The islands
The people living on the islands off the mainland of Spain are also proud of their heritage. There are about half a million inhabitants on the Balearic Islands, the vast majority on Mallorca. They are a mixture of all the peoples who roamed over the Mediterranean in early times. For centuries, the islanders lived on fishing and agriculture, until tourism changed their way of life dramatically. Their language is a slightly different version of

---

Flamenco
Most Spaniards see flamenco dancing and guitar-playing as exotic, although foreign tourists think them typically Spanish. Flamenco was brought to Andalusia from northern Europe by the gypsies, whom the tightly knit communities of southern Spain regarded as outsiders.

the Catalan people speak in Catalonia.

The Canary Islands became part of Spain at the beginning of the fifteenth century. The local population, called *Gaunches,* died out by the following century. For the past hundred years, the subtropical climate of the islands has made them a favorite spot for tourists. Visitors from northern Europe go there especially between January and March to escape the winter cold.

6   Living off the Land

Until quite recently, most Spaniards lived off the land. For historical reasons, Spain's different regions have different kinds of land ownership. In the north, the land has been divided into smaller pieces with the passing of generations, so that there are many farms, with each holding only a little land. This kind of farm is known as *minifundio*. Minifundio farming is unproductive and takes a lot of labor. Often a farming family only has enough land for a few animals and crops for its own needs. Recent governments have been trying to solve this problem by encouraging farmers to exchange land among themselves so that their fields are all next to each other to make larger properties. Governments have also tried to help farmers set up cooperatives, so that, as a group, they can buy machinery to work their land more effectively and join together to sell their produce.

As the south was reconquered from the Arabs between the thirteenth and fifteenth centuries, large tracts of land were given to the Spanish knights who helped in the fighting. Many of these huge estates, known as *latifundios*, are still owned by one family, who often have not farmed the land effectively, either. The landowners would collect rent from their tenant farmers and go away to live in Madrid or other cities, keeping their estates as hunting reserves. The government has taken over a number of these estates that have not been run productively.

In the past 30 years, there have also been

attempts to dam water in the mountain areas to help regulate the supply to the regions that need it. This has made farming more stable and reliable in many areas of Central Spain, but there is still a migration of people from the country to the towns, where they can earn more money.

Green Spain

Some of the richest land in Spain is in the northern Basque Provinces and Galicia. There is enough rainfall for thick grass to grow, which is used to feed herds of dairy cattle. Milk and cheese for the whole of Spain come from this area. A lot of corn is also grown, some of which is used to feed pigs and chickens. The climate in northern Spain is also ideal for apples, pears, chestnuts,

These low stone granaries, or horréos, *are a distinctive feature of the Galician countryside. They are used to store grain or animal fodder off the ground so that it will not get wet or be eaten by pests.*

51

and walnuts. These are either exported or made into jams and preserves in the region. The Pyrenees and the mountain slopes of northern Spain are also the center for the country's forest industry. Oak, pine, and other woods are used for timber, the extraction of resin, or the making of barrels for Spain's wine industry.

The secano

In Granada the land is often divided into several crops. The climate is generally dry and hot, so that crops that do well under these conditions, such as olives and corn, are widely grown.

The dry land, or *secano*, of the central Spanish plateau is mainly used for growing cereals. Where the soil is poorer, olive and cork oak trees take the place of wheat, rye, and oats. Goats, pigs, and sheep are allowed to graze over large areas of land that produce very little for their size. By the end of the eighteenth century, Spain, which had

once been "the granary of Rome," could not produce enough cereals to support its own population. Although the country has the capacity to be self-sufficient, it has imported large quantities of cereals ever since.

The vineyards of Spain

Almost ten percent of all agricultural land in Spain, about 4.2 million acres (1.7 million hectares), is given over to growing grapes. They can grow in the chalky soils of the central plateau because the vines have long roots that reach down for the moisture beneath. Grapes grow particularly well along the river valleys, where they are guaranteed some water. Spain is the third largest exporter of wine after France and Italy. The famous red wines of the Rioja region in the north are matured in barrels, like French Bordeaux wines. Other regions, like Catalonia and Valencia, produce white wines as well. Catalonia produces a sparkling wine similar to champagne, and the Basque country even has a green wine, called Chacoli. Since Spain entered the European Community, its wine-growers have been trying to reduce the number of ordinary table wines they produce in order to concentrate on improving their quality wines.

Olives and goats

Another traditional crop grown in the dry center of Spain is the olive. The stunted trees require little attention and grow in the poorest soils. About ten percent of the land is used for olive trees, and the olives are often still harvested by hand. In winter, laborers beat the trees with long

Sherry

One of Spain's most important exports is sherry. This fortified wine gets its name from the region in Andalusia where it is produced, around Jerez de la Frontera. Sherry is made by blending several wines together and adding a small amount of brandy. The sherry grapes are picked in September, then left to dry on rush mats out in the sun. After pressing, the juice is left to ferment for several months in barrels that are kept unsealed so that the air can reach the young sherry. This is what gives the mature sherry its distinctive taste. After the fermentation period, the barrels are sealed. Then they are stored in huge cellars, or *bodegas,* where the barrels are stacked in rows, with the oldest wine at the bottom, and the newest wine at the top.

Sherry is left to mature in these huge oak casks. They are kept in a cool bodega, *or wine store, with the barrels stacked one on top of each other.*

sticks to make the olives fall onto nets on the ground. After harvesting, the olives are mostly pressed to extract the oil, of which Spain is the world's largest producer. Where no crops at all can be planted, people often keep herds of goats and sheep for their meat, wool, milk, and cheese. They let the animals roam in search of their own food, and herdsmen often spend weeks away from their villages tending them.

Intensive farming
Over the past few years, the coastal strip of the south of Spain has seen the rise of intensive farming. Here, often under plastic, the high temperatures and rich soil help produce flowers and fruits like strawberries and melons even in winter and early spring. Spain exports these crops to the countries of northern Europe, where they sell for high prices. These exports earn important sums of foreign currency, but people

In recent years, parts of the southern coast of Spain have been called the "Costa del Plastic." Huge areas have been covered by plastic greenhouses that are used to grow soft fruit all year round. Thanks to the warmth under plastic and regular supplies of water, this semidesert region can produce strawberries and other fruits, which are exported to supermarkets all over Europe.

are now concerned that the soil in the region may be suffering from overuse by this intensive method of farming.

The Mediterranean garden

The coastal strip of the Eastern Mediterranean side of Spain is also very fertile. Since the days of Arab rule, water from the rivers flowing down from the mountains has been used to irrigate fields where fruits such as oranges, lemons, and figs are grown. The Arabs also brought almond trees with them. The Spaniards still grow almonds extensively and sell them for export to many countries.

The region around Valencia is known as the *huerta,* or "the garden of Spain." It is very beautiful in spring, with mile after mile of orange trees in blossom. People have drained the marshland of the coast and irrigated it to grow rice. In the hotter areas, they also grow tobacco and cotton.

Spanish farming and the European Community

Since joining the European Community in 1986, Spanish agriculture has had to face competition from Italy, France, and Portugal, which grow similar produce. The Spanish government is encouraging attempts to improve quality and make farming more productive. It is trying to advance the idea of agriculture as an industry that must be more modern and efficient if it is to feed the nation and earn money from exports. One result of the government's efforts is the increasing amount of land where people grow sunflowers for oil, or sugar beets, for sugar.

Fishing the seas

The Spaniards have always been great fishermen, catching sardines, tuna, mackerel, cod, and other white fish all around the long Spanish coastline. From Galacia and the Basque Provinces, they have ventured out into the Atlantic for cod and other deep-sea fish. Boats from the Canary Islands have made excellent catches off the coast of Africa. Anchovies and shellfish are caught in the calmer waters of the Mediterranean. The importance of fishing is reflected in the many canning factories along the coasts, and also in the rich fish recipes that are typical of the cooking of much of Spain's coastal region.

In recent years, fishing has gone into a decline. The Spanish fishing fleet is somewhat old and the industry is based on small family units. In the mid-1980s, almost a third of Spain's 17,000 fishing boats were judged to be improperly equipped for the needs of modern fishing. Since joining the European Community, Spain has been asked to cut the size of its fishing fleet still further.

7   Industry and Energy

One of the attractions that drew the Phoenicians to Spain over 2,000 years ago was the tin mined there. Ever since, Spain's mines and mining industry have been very important to the country's economy. The main deposits of iron ore are in the northern Basques Provinces, so they are the center for iron and steel making. Bilbao is the main port for the industry. In 1989, Spain

The mines at Rio Tinto have been in use since the Phoenicians arrived 2,500 years ago. Deposits of copper ore and sulfur lie near the surface and are scooped out with giant diggers.

produced over 11 million tons of steel. The richest coal deposits are in the Asturias. Asturian coal is now used in the iron industry, although for many years it was cheaper to import coal from Wales to Bilbao. Asturian coal also powers many of Spain's electric power stations.

There are other large mines in the south of the country. Since the last century, a British company has owned the Rio Tinto copper mine near Huelva, and so some of the villages near the open mine look exactly like mining villages in Britain. In nearby Andalusia, there are lead mines. The world's largest mercury mine is at Almadén, near Ciudad Real. Nearly all of this mercury is exported to the United States. Spain is also a major producer of cement, much of which is exported.

Shipbuilding

Another traditional heavy industry in Spain is shipbuilding. When Spain had a vast empire, there was a great demand for ships. Most of the shipyards are on the Atlantic coast, especially at El Ferrol and Cádiz. Today, Spain's shipbuilders make anything from fishing boats to oil tankers. As in many countries, however, Spain's shipbuilding industry has been in crisis since the end of the 1970s. There is not enough demand for ships, and many firms and workers have left the industry.

Cars

The most recent use for steel has been in the production of cars and trucks. Madrid and Barcelona are the centers of the car industry, although Ford has a giant factory near Valencia that produces about 250,000 cars a year. There are no Spanish car manufacturers left, and all cars manufactured there are made by foreign companies. The best-established of these is Seat, which is owned by the German company, Volkswagen. The French firms Citröen and Renault also have large factories in Spain.

Food, leather, and ceramics

Until recently, Spain was, above all, an agricultural country. Much of its industry was based on producing food, using animal hides or wool to make clothes, and canning fish and fruit. These activities, as well as the wine industry, are still important all over the country. Every region

The tradition of making colorful pottery was started by the Arabs. Many villages have their own designs and colors, which have remained similar for hundreds of years.

has its local delicacies and crafts. Leather goods are made in Toledo and Valencia, and the Balearic Islands have a busy shoemaking industry.

The wool from sheep and goats kept on the slopes of the Pyrenees helped Catalonia start a textile industry. Swift rivers flowing down to the Mediterranean proved useful in providing energy to spin cotton. The textile industry expanded rapidly at the end of the 1800s, with Barcelona as its most important sales and export center. Barcelona also became the center for the fashion industry, rivaling Milan in Italy.

The ceramic industry is another one that goes back hundreds of years. The Moors who ruled Spain were experts at making pottery and brightly colored tiles, and the tradition continues to this day. Many villages and small towns produce their own distinctive kind of pottery. Around Seville and Valencia, there are larger ceramic factories. The firm of Manises, near Valencia, produces tiles that are world-famous.

Tourism
Today, tourism is one of the main industries in Spain. Tourism was promoted in the 1950s as a way of bringing much-needed foreign currency into the country. By the early 1960s, there were 10 million visitors to Spain every year. Now, there are over 50 million, and most of them come from other West European countries or the U.S.

At the start of the tourism boom, the Spaniards built hundreds of hotels along the south and east coasts, as well as on the Balearic and Canary islands. Many fishing villages rapidly changed beyond recognition. Many of the resorts catered

It was in the 1960s that Spain first developed tourism on its coast. The tourists, mostly from northern Europe, brought with them foreign currency that was crucial for Spain's development. Many people now feel that the Spanish coast, especially in the Mediterranean and the Balearic Islands, was badly spoiled by all the cheap hotels that were built quickly to accommodate tourists.

to vacationers on cheap package tours. Neither the local authorities nor the developers paid much attention to planning or to the effects that this rapid expansion and so many people would have on the environment. As a result, some of the Mediterranean coastline has been spoiled forever, including historic towns like Seville, Toledo, and Segovia.

Spain depends very heavily on its tourist industry, though. Tourists bring the equivalent of $1.7 billion into Spain's economy each year. Tourism provides work for two million Spaniards, not just in services for tourists, but in the building, farming and travel sectors, to name just a few. The Spanish government runs a number of high-class hotels, or *paradores*, throughout the country. These, often converted

Trading partners
At the end of the civil war, Spain was cut off from the outside world and did not sell much abroad. This has changed a great deal in the past 25 years, and Spain is now one of the most important trading nations in the world. Since joining the EC, about 66 percent of all goods imported and exported are to other European countries. West Germany, France, and Italy are Spain's main trading partners; Britain and the U.S. are less important. Many of Spain's industries still rely on small-scale factories that employ less than 50 people. This will have to change if Spain is to compete in the 1990s, since larger factories can produce goods more cheaply and efficiently.

The changes of the past 25 years have not been easy for Spain. Many thousands of people have had to move to where the new industries are, and this has caused housing problems and social tensions. Unemployment is widespread, especially in the rural areas where there is no longer any work on the land. Up to one in five Spaniards has no regular job.

palaces or castles, combine a sense of the past with all of today's comforts.

Energy problems
The development of energy resources to match the growth of industry has also been a problem in Spain. The only deposits of coal are in the north. The forests of wood that can be used for fuel are also there. Spain's rivers flowing west to the Atlantic are not rapid enough to provide power, so the coal and oil needed for generating

In recent years Spain has been harnessing the flow of water from its many mountains to make hydroelectricity. This is a control tower for a dam at Canale, near Granada. The dam was built in the 1980s across the Genil River.

electricity must be imported. A state-owned company deals with all the oil imports.

In recent years, Spain has started a huge program of building dams to generate energy. The water stored is used to produce almost 30 percent of the country's electricity. In the early 1980s, Spain decided to make nuclear power its main source of energy because it could mine its own uranium and produce the electricity cheaply. Ten nuclear plants have been built so far. These supply over 20 percent of Spain's electricity. Recently, an accident caused the government to rethink how much it wanted to depend on nuclear energy. There have been a few experiments using other kinds of energy, like solar power, from Spain's most readily available energy source, the sun.

8   Transportation and Communications

Road transportation has always been difficult in Spain. Its links with the rest of Europe are across the Pyrenees by means of mountain roads, which are often blocked by snow in winter. Within Spain, the high plateau and the mountain ranges rising from it have also made links by road a problem. Spain has the highest road in Europe, which reaches a height of almost 11,500 feet (3,469 meters) in the Sierra Nevada in Andalusia.

The Romans were the first to build good roads throughout the country, as they did in most of

The Talgo, Spain's fast train, approaches Córdoba station on its run from Madrid to Seville.

Europe. Some of these roads are still in use today. For many centuries after Roman rule was over, the roads of Spain were neglected and unsafe. Even well into the last century, a journey to Madrid from any other main city was a great adventure. It was dangerous because of the many bands of robbers who lived in the mountains and attacked travelers in their coaches.

Spanish railroads
The coming of the railroads in the second half of the last century brought Spain's communications

The railroad system in Madrid was modernized in the 1980s. It is now fast and efficient and is used by many thousands of people every day to get from the outlying suburbs to work in the center of the city.

network together. The railroad system now covers some 7,460 miles (12,000 kilometers). Its center is Madrid, where the line for each main region ends at a different station. The railroad network is known as the RENFE (Red Nacional de los Ferrocarriles Españoles). Spanish railroads have a wider track than French ones, which means that international trains crossing the border either have to change the width of their wheel axles, or the passengers have to change trains.

Although there are some excellent fast trains, like the Talgo, named after the Basque engineer who invented it, RENFE has a poor reputation in Spain. Train rides are slow, often because there is only one track, so trains cannot run in opposite directions at the same time. The slowest trains, which stop everywhere, are known as *tranvías*. Other kinds of trains are the *semi-directos*, which stop in fewer places, the *rápidos* and the *expresos* which, in spite of their names, are not high-speed. In 1987, the government announced an ambitious plan for modernizing the railroads and creating more fast intercity services.

Only Madrid and Barcelona have subway systems. People pay a flat fare for all rides, like on the Parisian metro. In 1988, the first section of a subway was opened in Valencia, and Bilbao and Seville may also have subways in time for the World Fair in 1992.

Highways and traffic jams
Over the past 30 years, roads have regained their importance in Spain. By the mid-1980's, 90 percent of all passenger trips were made by road, and 75 percent of all goods were carried by truck.

A new program of road-building has been undertaken, with highways, called *autopistas,* linking the main cities. The government is also building main roads and plans to have 9,320 miles (15,000 kilometers) of new road by 1992.

The main roads of Spain radiate from the Puerta del Sol in Madrid. There are six of them, each of which has a Roman numeral. The N I goes from Madrid to Santander, the N II to Barcelona, the N III to Valencia, the N IV to Cádiz, the N V to Badajoz, and the N VI to LaCoruña. There are still problems traveling across Spain. It is only in coastal areas, where the roads have been built for tourists, that they are really adequate.

There are now well over 10 million cars in Spain—one for every four inhabitants. Anyone

Like many old cities, Madrid cannot cope with the volume of cars in its center. Highways have been built to carry as much traffic as possible, but the old parts of the city still have atascos, *or traffic jams, in the morning and evening.*

over 18 can hold a driver's license. The poor roads, the mountains, and the fact that many Spaniards love to drive very fast all account for the high rate of accidents. The government is trying to combat this by making the use of seat belts compulsory and penalizing drunk drivers.

Traffic has become a great problem for Spain's old cities. Their narrow streets cannot cope with the number of cars used by people driving to work or the stores each day. Many Spaniards like to drive home at midday for lunch, then back to work again, so that there are four "rush hours" each day. Many historic towns have now closed their main squares to traffic and introduced pedestrian-only areas. They have also created "blue zones," where people must have special permits in order to park. A red and white stripe on a curb means no parking is allowed at all, and most cities have very efficient traffic police to make sure people obey the regulations.

Sea links

Spain's road links with the rest of Europe have so many difficulties that sea routes are all the more vital. Spain's Mediterranean ports have always traded with Italy and the eastern Mediterranean. Galicia has close links across the Bay of Biscay with Britain and the northwest of Europe. Seventy-five percent of Spain's foreign trade still depends on ships There are almost 500 ships in Spain's merchant fleet, but this is not nearly enough to cope with all the trade from Spanish ports. There are also important ferry services to the Balearic Islands from Barcelona and Valencia, and to Britain from Santander.

Airlines
Tourism has been a great spur to the airline industry. There are now international flights to all Spain's main coastal resorts, and 40 cities have airports. Spaniards frequently travel by air within their country, because of the relatively long distances between the major cities and the poor roads and slow trains. There is a shuttle service every hour between Madrid and Barcelona, and there are frequent flights to the Balearic and Canary islands.

Spain's main airline is named Iberia, after the ancient name for the country. The company was set up in 1940 and nationalized in 1943. Iberia now flies to almost 100 destinations all around the world. There are also several large Spanish charter air companies that deal with the enormous summer influx of tourists from all over Europe.

Spain has few deep rivers or canals, so its internal waterways are only some 186 miles (300 kilometers) long. Seville is the only major inland port, exporting mainly olives and fruit. Barcelona is the country's largest port, followed by Valencia and Málaga on the Mediterranean, Vigo and Cádiz on the Atlantic, and Bilbao and Gijón on the north coast.

Postal service and telecommunications
The Spanish postal service, like the railroads, has a reputation for not being very efficient, especially in rural areas. People can buy stamps at post offices, but also at cigar shops, as in France. This is because the state runs both the postal

The main post office in Madrid is one of the city's landmarks. It is on the corner of the Prado, the shady avenue that also contains the capital's most famous museum.

service and cigar and cigarette production. Spanish mailboxes are bright yellow. The Franco regime neglected the telephone system. Now, Spain is trying to modernize it and extend the network to more people. While a great many Spanish homes now have a telephone, phone calls to many rural areas are still connected through an operator.

TV and radio

TV and radio are important means of keeping in touch in a large country like Spain, with many isolated regions. Until recently, all Spanish television was run by a state-owned corporation, Radiotelevisión Española (RTVE). RTVE now runs two daily television channels and the state radio system. New laws at the end of the 1980s allowed private companies to operate on three new television channels. A new body called Retevisión (Red Técnica Española de Televisión) will run this new system. Besides the national channels, many of the autonomous regions have their own TV stations, often broadcasting in the local language. In recent years, satellite and cable television have also become available in the big cities. In 1987, estimates showed that there were over 14 million television sets in Spain, and slightly fewer radios.

The press

The written press was closely controlled under the Franco regime. With the return of democracy in the late 1970s, there was a great boom, with all kinds of daily newspapers and weekly magazines being published. Some of these did not last very long, but Spain still issues 105 different newspapers a day. The main newspapers are published in Madrid. The best-selling newspaper is *El País*. Other large circulation papers are *Diario 16, El Periódico, La Vanguardia*, and *Ya*. Private companies own them, but the papers are usually sympathetic to a particular political party. Spain still has a strong regional press, and many people buy the small daily and weekly newspapers it produces.

9 The Spanish Way of Life

Spain's history has given the Spaniards a special way of life. Their past affects the way they think, what they believe, and how they behave. It influences the way they educate their children, and how they regard the government.

The Spanish state
Spaniards often regard the forces behind their government with suspicion. The civil war and the Franco regime have left many people with the idea that the military forces are against democracy. In the 1980s, this feeling gradually changed as more of the old officers retired and the army became more professional. As head of the armed forces, King Juan Carlos helped enormously in this. Even today, though, many Spaniards have to do 15 months military service when they are 19. This can be postponed if they are in school.

Besides the armed forces, Spaniards also distrust their politicians. Democracy has now

---

Currency
The Spanish unit of money is the *peseta*. Up to 100 pesetas, the money is in coins, and sums over 100 pesetas are paper money. The denominations of paper money all show famous writers, except for the 5,000-peseta note, which has a portrait of King Juan Carlos.

returned to Spain, and there are regular elections and stable, legal political parties with moderate beliefs. However, many Spaniards still argue fiercely about politics. Although a left- wing party has been in power for the last decade, there is no talk of trying to make Spain a republic again, so perhaps most Spaniards are content with the kind of constitutional monarchy they now have.

The police

Spaniards are also very wary of their police. There are three different police forces in Spain, all of them armed. The most numerous are the *policia nacional*. They wear brown uniforms and enforce law and order in towns and cities. Helping them are the *policia municipal*, in blue, who control

This woman in Laujaron in the Sierra Nevada is part of the policia municipal, *or traffic police. It is only recently that women have been able to have such jobs.*

traffic and deal with minor crimes. Thirdly, there are the *guardia civil*. They wear green uniforms, but are more recognizable by their traditional shiny black hats. They patrol Spain's frontiers, roads, and countryside and play a strong part in regional disputes and controlling demonstrations, making them the police force Spaniards dislike most.

Religion
The Catholic Church has always been a strong force in shaping Spanish society. Since the days of Ferdinand and Isabella 500 years ago, Spaniards have seen themselves as defenders of the true faith. According to the 1978 constitution, Catholicism is no longer the state religion as such, but the vast majority of Spaniards are Catholic, at least in name. There are over 60,000 Catholic churches in Spain, as well as many monasteries and convents run by different religious orders. Spain continues to send many missionaries to Latin America, Africa, and the Far East.

About one in every five Spaniards attends mass regularly, although this number is falling rapidly as fewer young people keep up the tradition. Most Spaniards still believe in getting married and baptizing their children in church. Many take part in the traditional religious festivals celebrated throughout the year, especially at Christmas, in the week before Easter, and at the start of November to pray for the dead.

The local parish priest still has a lot of influence, particularly in rural areas. The Church plays an important role in education, and, as in other European countries, women make up most of the

Traditional Christian beliefs are evident in most Spanish towns during Holy Week, or Semana Santa, before Easter. In Seville, men dress as penitents from the time of the Inquisition. They form processions to carry heavy wooden biers bearing statues of Christ, the Virgin Mary, or one of the saints. These statues are dressed in velvet and silk and decked with jewels. Each year there is great rivalry between the different churches of Seville for the most beautiful bier.

faithful and are the ones most influenced by pressure from the Church. Divorce only became legal in Spain in 1981, and the Catholic Church still resists the dissolution of marriages.

The second biggest religious group in Spain is the Muslims, of whom there are 300,000. There are only 30,000 registered Protestants, and as few as 12,000 practicing Jews.

Welfare and health

Spain's health service is struggling to match that of its European neighbors. Those Spaniards who can afford to use private doctors and dentists. Public health care is spread very unevenly through the country. There are few doctors in the rural areas, and services have not been able to keep up with the large-scale movement of the population to large towns and cities. Diseases like tuberculosis and typhoid, which do not appear now in the rest of Europe, still occur in Spain, as does severe malnutrition.

The social security system in Spain, which provides money to help old people and those who are unemployed or sick, is also inadequate. State pensions in Spain are very low, and most

Traditionally, Spanish families have been large, so when there is a wedding, there is usually a large number of guests. Family life is seen as very important in Spain.

people who have no job find that they are not entitled to any money or benefits at all. This is mainly because the government does not have enough money in its social security budget to pay them.

More than in other European countries, Spanish women have traditionally stayed at home to look after the family. It is only in the past ten years that they have been demanding jobs and equal rights with men. The first woman firefighter, for example, was only appointed in 1990. Men are still very much the dominant sex in Spanish society, but many young women, especially in the big cities, have protested this, and things are gradually changing. In 1985, for example, it became legal to have an abortion on health grounds. Despite this legislation, many doctors in Spain still refuse to carry out abortions because they think it is morally wrong.

Family life
The family is a stronger unit in Spain than it is in many other Western European countries. This is due to the Catholic tradition, the dominant role of the men, and the way old or unemployed people rely on their families, not the state, for help. Lots of city dwellers live in apartments known as *pisos.* These apartments usually have a formal dining-room, used only on Sundays and special occasions, and a living room, where the family usually meets. The kitchen usually has fewer gadgets than in the United States.

Spaniards like to have apartments in the center of town. The cities, however, are ringed with apartment buildings that were built in a hurry

Spanish Names
Every Spaniard has two surnames. The first of these comes from his or her father, the second from the mother. In theory, when a woman marries, she takes her husband's two names and adds them to her own two, with the preposition *de*. So if María González Castillo marries a man called Pedro Ramírez García, she would officially become María González Castillo de Ramírez García. Her letters would be addressed to María Ramírez González and her children would also have these two names. Increasingly, the Spaniards are following the rest of Europe and just using one surname—the father's.

when the industrial boom of the 1960s drew thousands of people from the countryside. These "dormitory towns" where city workers eat and sleep are unpopular because they were often badly planned and have few amenities. Many families have kept links with the countryside, which they visit on weekends, or holidays, especially during the long summer break. Spaniards often have closer ties with the village or region they left behind than they do with the city where they work.

Traditionally, Spanish families are large. The idea of having only one or two children has only become more common in the last decade. Even so, Spaniards feel that they belong to an "extended family" where aunts, uncles, grandparents, and cousins either live in the same house or nearby and see each other frequently. This is not common in northern Europe. Spanish families get together on weekends or on national feast days and celebrate with a meal. Spanish young people, especially girls, often live at home until they get married. Even after their marriage, they often live close to their family.

Education
Education has also changed a lot in the past generation. Even in the 1960s, less than half of

These schoolchildren have been taken on a school outing to the historic town of Toledo to study Spanish history.

Spain's children stayed at school until they were 14. They left to start work instead, especially those who lived in the countryside. Since 1970, schooling has been compulsory in Spain for all children between the ages of 6 and 14. A small proportion of parents send their children to private kindergartens from the age of two. Even more parents send their four-year-olds to nursery schools, but the majority of Spanish children still have their first experience of school at age six.

These Spanish school girls in Cádiz are taking part in a fiesta. In Spain, schoolchildren have a long day, but they also have long vacations and days off for fiestas. They enjoy taking part in the celebrations.

Spanish state schools for children from 6 to 14 years are called Centros de Educacíon General Básica (CEGBs). The eight years of school are split into two parts, the first from 6 to 11, and the second from12 to 14, and lead to a final certificate. Pupils have to repeat any year of schooling in which they get bad grades.

School starts at 9 A.M.. There is a break for lunch between 1 P.M. and 3 P.M. when those who can go home for lunch do so. Then there are more classes until 5 P.M.. This makes the school day very long for Spanish children, but their vacations are long as well. They have up to three months' break in the summer, two to three weeks at Christmas, two weeks at Easter, and several feast days. Most schools are still single sex. Two-thirds of Spanish children go to state schools and one-third to private ones, most of which are run by the Catholic Church.

After the age of 14, Spanish children either start vocational training *(formación professional)* or go on to an *instituto* to study for their *bachillerato,* which they take when they are 17. They can then do a year's preparation for the university, the Curso de Orientación Universitaria (COU), when they take the subjects they would like to study.

Universities
Nearly a million Spanish youngsters go to the university. Most study medicine or law. Not enough enroll for science subjects or social sciences. University teaching is still very traditional, with lectures to large numbers of students. There are 16 state universities, but over 25 percent of Spanish students go to the ones in Madrid or Barcelona. There are also 12 *universidades laborales,* which are polytechnic schools, where students take more vocational courses in applied sciences, engineering, journalism, and accounting. There are also several private universities and one that teaches by mail, radio, and television.

Problems of city life

Youngsters in Spain's cities share the problems of their counterparts everywhere in Europe. There is a lot of unemployment, so many of them cannot find work. The apartment buildings they live in offer little beyond somewhere to eat and sleep because they were badly planned. Their families often put a lot of pressure on them, which makes them rebel. Drug-taking and homelessness have become serious problems among Spanish young people.

10   Leisure and Pleasure

Spaniards take their pleasure as seriously as their work. They like to eat, talk, go out, and have fun together. The rhythm of daily life in Spain is quite different from that in the United States. Most people now work in towns or cities. The land is often farmed by the older generations. The large estates employ few laborers. In the towns, work starts early, but there is usually a break of several hours in the middle of the day. After a light breakfast of coffee, or hot chocolate with toast, bread, or *churros,* doughnut dough fried in horseshoe shapes, people are hungry by midday. Most Spaniards return home for lunch, which is often a very large meal. Many people, especially

Spaniards have a fondness for sweets. This buñuelo, *or doughnut stall, is similar to many that are found at fairs, markets, or on the streets during fiestas. A variety of cakes are sold.*

An Example of a School Menu

Lunes	*Monday*
Patatas con costillas	Potatoes with ribs
Huevos a la riojana con jamón	Eggs (Rioja style) with ham
Postre: Fruta del tiempo y leche	Dessert: Fruit of the season—milk
Martes	*Tuesday*
Puré de verduras	Vegetable puree
Estofado de carne con patatas	Meat stew with potatoes
Postre: Fruta del tiempo y leche	Dessert: Fruit of the season—milk
Miercoles	*Wednesday*
Arroz blanco con tomate	White rice with tomato
Merluza a la romana con ensalada	Fish with salad
Postre: Fruta del tiempo y leche	Dessert: Fruit of the season—milk
Jueves	*Thursday*
Macarrones a la italiana	Italian style macaroni
Empanadillas y croquetas caseras con ensalada	Meat pies and homemade croquettes with salad
Postre: Fruta del tiempo y leche	Dessert: Fruit of the season—milk
Viernes	*Friday*
Sopa de ave con estrellas	Chicken soup
Pollo asado con patatas fritas	Roast chicken and fries
Postre: Yogurt	Dessert: Yogurt

those in the countryside, have a short nap, or *siesta*, after lunch, particularly in the hot summer months.

At 4:30 or 5 P.M., Spaniards go back to work. In the past in order to make more money, many people had two jobs, one in the morning, and another in the late afternoon. In the 1980s, to help reduce unemployment, the government encouraged people to work only in one place. In offices and businesses, they have to work another two or three hours, which means that they get home quite late in the evening. Spaniards do not usually have their evening meal before 9 P.M. although the children will usually have been given a snack earlier. Evening entertainments, like the movies and the theater, start even later, at 10 or 10:30 P.M.. Often after the performance people will go to have coffee or a drink around midnight in a local cafe. This way of life is very traditional and hard to change, although many firms would like their employees to work a continuous day as their counterparts do in other European countries.

Spanish cooking
Spanish cuisine is one of the most varied in the world. It includes spices and flavors from Spain's Arab tradition. It uses many ingredients from its rich wildlife, and also from the worldwide empire that Spain once ruled. Spanish cuisine consists of generous helpings of meat, fish, and eggs and delicious sauces that people eat with a lot of crusty bread. Other specialties include game and ham. Cooks in Spain know how to get the best out of everything. So, for example, one of the delicacies of Madrid is tripe cooked *a la Madrileña*. Olive oil is the basis for most Spanish dishes, and each town and region has its own favorites. *Paella* is a typical Valencian dish of rice, seafood and chicken. A heavy meat stew called *cocido* is typical of Castille, while salt cod, or *bacalao* is a delicacy on the northern coast. A number of foods, like chocolate, potatoes, pepper, and tomatoes, were brought to Spain from its colonies in the Americas and have become an integral part not only of Spanish but European cookery. A Spaniard is

Zarzuela
The zarzuela is a kind of Spanish romantic operetta, which is very popular in Madrid and other large cities. The zarzuelas are often based on regional folk tales and include songs, dances, and comedy. They are also very popular on television.

said to have invented tomato sauce centuries ago, when he cooked one of the strange new vegetables with olive oil and onions.

The Arab cooking tradition gave Spaniards a taste for very sweet things. They like to eat quince jelly, or *dulce de membrillo* with cheese from the province of La Mancha as a dessert. Another favorite at Christmas is *turrón*, a kind of candy made from almonds and sugar paste. On Twelfth Night, Epiphany, which is still the traditional time to give children their presents, Spaniards eat a circular cake decorated with cream and crystallized fruits. It is called the *Roscón de Reyes* (King's Crown). The cake contains a lucky charm, and whoever gets the piece containing it becomes king or queen for the evening.

Going out
In the country, many Spaniards like to go out and hunt, particularly on weekends. Otherwise, there is often little to do in the country villages, except when it is time for a celebration, or fiesta. In the towns, Spaniards enjoy going out a lot. They are regular movie-goers, watching films by well-known Spanish directors like Luís Berlanga, Carlos Saura, or the young Pedro Almodóvar. In

Taking a walk in the streets of towns or villages is a very popular pastime in Spain, especially in the evening. Here people are strolling along the Ramblas, a wide pedestrian thoroughfare in Barcelona.

cities, they also like to go to the theater, though there are few theaters left now in the smaller towns. On the weekends, many people visit art galleries and museums to enjoy the glories of Spain's past. Spain has always produced great painters, from Velázquez, Murillo, and Goya to Pablo Picasso, Joan Miró, and Salvador Dalí.

In the early evening, it is common for Spanish men to get together for a drink and talk over the affairs of the day. Older men make a habit of this *tertulia*, or gathering, when few if any women are present. The simple pleasure of the evening walk, or *paseo*, around the main square is still widespread in many of Spain's smaller towns and villages. Young adults all over Spain enjoy an occasional rock concert or they go out to bars for a drink or to clubs to dance. Spain's bars are lively, noisy places, and Spaniards enjoy visiting them to drink coffee, sherry, or wine and to eat *tapas*. *Tapas* are plates of small snacks that can vary from pieces of squid or octopus to different kinds of sausages, olives, or salads. Often someone in the bar will play a guitar, and others will sing.

Bullfighting and other sports
On weekends, Spanish families like to get together. They often go back to their village. Some go to church, and all of them meet for the main meal which is on Sunday around midday. Sunday afternoons are the time for sports, or for some to go to the opera or *zarzuela*. In the summer months, the typical sport is bullfighting, while in the winter thousands of people go to soccer matches. Bullfights, or *corridas*, are often seen as the essence of Spanish life, but they have been losing their popularity in recent years. Spaniards see the matador's killing of the bull in the ring as an art, in which the man is risking his life. They appreciate the courage and strength of the bull and praise the man for his grace and ability to overcome brute force with style. In bullfighting, the Spanish idea of honor, for both man and animal, is expressed in its highest form.

The Spaniards' other main sporting passion is soccer. The major teams like Real Madrid or FC Barcelona have immense stadiums, where 50,000 people turn out every Sunday to see their team perform in the Spanish Leagues or in the annual cup competition. Spanish teams are among the best in Europe, and the national team is among the best in the world.

In pelota the ball can travel at speeds of up to 185 miles per hour (300 kilometers per hour), making pelota an extremely fast and dangerous game.

Pelota

This game from the Basque Provinces is the fastest game in the world. Players can play in singles or doubles, in which case there are four players in teams of two. Each player holds a curved basket, or *cesta*, in one hand and uses it to fling a small, hard ball against the front wall of the court, trying to angle his shot so that his opponent cannot return it. In the Basque areas there are professional players. The Spaniards have taken this game across the Atlantic. In Latin America and the United States it is called jai alai.

Another popular sport is basketball. There are many surprisingly tall Spaniards among the younger generations, and basketball clubs also import players from the United States to play for them. Cycling also has a strong following. The Tour of Spain is one of the major international competitions each year, and Spain regularly produces very good riders. In the winter, many people like to go skiing in the Pyrenees, the Cantabrian Mountains, or the Sierra Nevada.

For many years, school sports were neglected. Once again, this is something that has been changing in this generation. Children now get much more exercise, and there is more emphasis on all Spaniards being healthy. Spaniards are still among the heaviest smokers in Europe, as the state-run tobacco industry produces cheap cigarettes. The Spanish diet is also rather rich and not very balanced.

Fiestas

Spain is a country of *fiestas,* those public celebrations held outside where everyone joins in. Fiestas can be huge affairs involving thousands of people, or small gatherings in villages. In addition to national holidays, each town annually celebrates its own patron saint's day. Other fiestas last for a week, like the Feria in Seville or the San Fermín celebrations in Pamplona. There is a week of rejoicing, with dancing and signing traditional dances and songs in the streets. There is also a tradition to release bulls along the main street each day. Many young people run in front of them, to show their courage. The *Vendimia,* or grape harvest, usually takes place around October.

91

11 Looking to the Future

For much of its history, Spain has been cut off from the rest of Europe. Even in this century its isolation continued because of the civil war and the Franco regime. Spain seemed so distant to other Europeans that it was often known as "Africa beyond the Pyrenees."

The situation has changed a great deal in the past 30 years. By the late 1980s, Spain had become a member of developed Western Europe. Like its neighbors, it enjoys a stable parliamentary democracy, with a monarchy similar to those that have proved so enduring in Britain and the Netherlands. There is violence in the Basque

These posters were designed to publicize the Olympic Games of 1992, to be held in Barcelona. These two posters by Antoni Tapies and Enric Satue were joint prizewinners with two others. The four posters were circulated worldwide to publicize the games.

The Crown Prince
King Juan Carlos's son Felipe, the heir to the Spanish throne, was born on January 30, 1968. He was given the traditional title of Prince of Asturias, in the same way as the heir to the British throne is called the Prince of Wales. Although Spain has twice been a republic, most Spaniards are now in favor of rule by constitutional monarchs. Even the Socialist party agrees and supports the king and his heirs.

There are still strong separatist movements among the Spanish, particularly among the Basques and Catalans. These red scarves and hats worn during the fiesta of San Fermín in Pamplona show the Basque people's loyalty to their region.

region, but there are similar problems in other European countries and there seems to be no easy solution. The basis of Spain's economy has changed from agriculture to industry, and its population now lives mostly in towns and cities.

It plays a full role in the European Community and is now part of the NATO defense organization as well.

The challenge that faces Spain in the 1990s is to continue its integration into Europe without sacrificing its own traditions and way of life. Much of Spain's countryside is now almost deserted, and farming needs to be made more profitable so that people will not continue to drift away from the land. The government has to find ways of encouraging the young, in particular, not to leave Andalusia and the south for the big towns of the north. The government also needs to do more to encourage young people in the towns to lead independent and useful lives. Young women especially have to be given more chances to work outside the home and to succeed in professions. The state could perhaps promote more industry in the south and organize agriculture there more efficiently.

Spain will continue to be one of the world's most important tourist centers. However, the country must plan what it needs first and make sure that there is no more harm done to its coasts, cities, and environment generally.

As the twenty-first century approaches, Spain looks back on its 500-year relationship with the Americas. It may be that its role in the future will continue to be as a link between Europe and the Western Hemisphere.

Index

Inquisition 22–23
irrigation 10, 12, 56
Isabella and Ferdinand 22–23, 25, 75
isolation 5, 25, 36, 92

Juan Carlos, King 37–39, 73

land use 31, 50–51, 94
language 14, 20, 42–46, 49
literature 21, 26

Madrid 15, 25, 33, 41–43, 59, 67–68
Mallorca 7, 48
Mediterranean Sea 7, 14–15, 57, 62
Menorca 7, 27
migration 15, 36–37, 48, 51, 63, 77
military service 73
mining and minerals 58–59, 63
mountains 8, 10, 11, 65, 91
movies and theater 86–88
music 47, 49, 87, 89

national parks 12, 14
nuclear power 64

oil 63–64
olives 11, 17, 52–53, 55, 87

parliament (Cortes Generales) 39
Philip II 27, 42
Philippines 24, 29, 30
Phoenicians 12–13, 17, 58
plant life 10–12
police 74–75
population 15, 30, 42–43, 48

ports 20, 25, 47, 58, 70
Pyrenees 5, 45, 52, 61, 65, 91

religion 18–20, 22–25, 27, 36, 75–76
    Christianity 18, 22, 24, 75–76
    Islam 19, 20, 23, 76
Republic 30–34, 44
rivers 8–9, 63
Romans 17–18, 43, 65–66

Santiago de Compostela 22
Seville 10, 20, 25, 43, 47, 62, 70
shipbuilding 59
sports 89–91
Suárez, Adolfo 38–39

television and radio 36, 43, 71–72
Tenerife 7
Toledo 42, 61–62
tourism 10, 48–49, 61–63, 94
trade unions 37–38
transportation 18, 42, 65–70

unemployment 63, 83, 85
urban life 15, 36–37, 78–79, 83

Valencia 14, 28, 30, 56, 59, 70
Vigo 47, 70

wildlife 12–14
wine production 11, 17, 52–54
women 74, 75, 78, 94
World War II 35–36